Written by Sarah Nathan
Based on an episode by Craig Gerber
Illustrated by Character Building Studio and the Disney Storybook Art Team

This edition published by Parragon Books Ltd in 2015

Parragon Books Ltd
Chartist House
15–17 Trim Street
Bath BA1 1HA, UK
www.parragon.com

ISBN 978-1-4748-1388-4

Printed in China

Sofia's Magic Lesson

Bath · New York · Cologne · Melbourne · Delhi
Hong Kong · Shenzhen · Singapore · Amsterdam

Sofia is so excited! It's her first sorcery class ever at Royal Prep. "I can't wait to learn magic," she says, taking her seat next to James in the classroom.

Fauna, their sorcery teacher, explains that the first lesson is a spell to change a rock into a ruby.

Sofia gets set to try the spell. She waves her wand, says the magic words, and turns her rock into... an apple! Oops!

Sofia looks around and sees that all the other kids have rubies on their desks. "Don't worry, class," says Fauna.

"You can practice at home later. We have three new spells to learn today." Three new spells – plus a test at the end of the week! How will Sofia ever learn them all?

After school, Sofia practices her spells with Clover. This time, she turns a rock into a tomato!

"It was supposed to turn into a ruby," she says, disappointed.

Clover grabs the tomato. "This is much better," he says, taking a big bite. "If you want to learn magic, ask a sorcerer!"

That's it! Cedric is just the person to help Sofia!

When Cedric sees Sofia at his door, he can't help staring at her magical amulet. "It's so nice to see your amulet – I mean, you," he quickly adds, inviting her inside.

As Sofia looks around at the mess in Cedric's workshop, she gets an idea. "Could I help clean up your workshop in return for magic lessons?" she asks.

Having Sofia in his workshop every day will give Cedric a chance to take the amulet! So he agrees to make Sofia his apprentice.

"I'm going to brew up a potion that will make me invisible," Cedric tells Wormwood after Sofia leaves. "Then I'll swipe Sofia's amulet and rule the kingdom!

"I will be King Cedric the First!" Cedric cries happily.

When Sofia returns the next day, she's ready for her first magic lesson. She cleans while Cedric works on his invisibility potion.
It doesn't go very well, though.

Poof!

Next Cedric teaches Sofia a phrase his father, Goodwyn the Great, taught him: "Slow and steady does the trick." Sofia holds her wand straight, and she slowly recites the magic words. It works! In her hand is a ruby!

"I did it!" Sofia exclaims. "You are a really good teacher, Mr. Cedric."

Cedric blushes. He's not used to getting compliments.

Just then, Baileywick comes in with a message for Cedric. King Roland wants to see him right away.

Roland tells Cedric that King Magnus is coming for a visit. "He's always bragging about his kingdom," King Roland says. He points to the stone gargoyles. "Maybe you could change the gloomy gargoyles into golden horses? That would impress him!"

So Cedric raises his wand and turns a gargoyle into a winged horse...but it flies away! King Roland shakes his head. "Not every royal sorcerer can be as gifted as your father," he says. Poor Cedric!

"Sorry your spell didn't work," says Sofia.
Cedric shrugs. Then he tells Sofia about his father
-- the greatest royal sorcerer who ever waved a wand.
"He even saved King Roland's father nine times! But I
haven't saved anyone's life."

Just then, one of the potion bottles falls off the shelf and turns Sofia into a lizard!

In an instant, Cedric leaps into action. "Lizardo chango!"

And— Poof!

Sofia changes back. "Thank you!" Sofia exclaims.

"Oh, that's an easy spell," Cedric says.

Sofia looks up at Cedric. "You're so good at magic. So why couldn't you turn the gargoyles into golden horses?"

Cedric admits that when he's around the king, he gets nervous.

"I'm going to find a way to show Dad that you're a great sorcerer," Sofia tells Cedric.

"Why would you do that?" Cedric asks.

Sofia grins. "Because you're my friend."

At dinner that night, King Magnus goes on and on about his kingdom and his sorcerer.

"We have a great sorcerer, too," Sofia says. "We should have him put on a show!" Her family looks worried. After all, Cedric isn't really great at magic. But when King Magnus finds out that Cedric is the son of Goodwyn the Great, he insists.

Back in Cedric's workshop, Sofia encourages her friend.

"We can help each other get ready," she says. "Remember: slow and steady does the trick." While Cedric is busy preparing tricks for his royal magic show, Sofia practices her spells for the sorcery test.

But her spells still aren't perfect.

A little later, as Sofia cleans Cedric's workshop, she wipes a smudge off his spell book and discovers why Cedric's invisibility potion isn't working! He didn't see two ingredients on the list!

When Sofia tells him the news, Cedric can't believe it! Now he can finally make the potion! He says good night to Sofia, drops the final two ingredients into the cauldron, and smiles. "I did it, Wormy!" he shouts. And then Cedric sees what Sofia left for him.

"She made this for me?" Cedric asks. Nobody has ever done anything like that for him before.

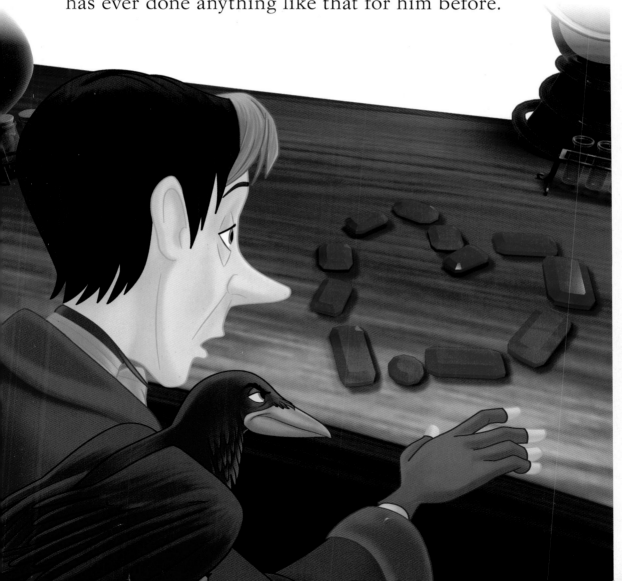

The next day, Sofia is ready for her magic test!
Fauna passes out a rock, a lime, and an old shoe.
"You must perform the three transformation spells
we learned this week," she says.
Sofia takes a deep breath and remembers Cedric's
advice. "Slow and steady," she tells herself.

It works! Sofia
passes the sorcery
test!
She runs home to
show Mum and
Dad her gold star.

Meanwhile, Cedric is ready for the magic show. "When it's time for my last trick, I'll pour the invisibility potion on myself, swipe Sofia's amulet, and take over the kingdom!" he tells Wormwood.

The magic show begins, and Cedric announces that his first trick will be to make Clover fly. But instead, he makes poor Clover bounce!

Sofia feels bad for Cedric. If only he were doing a trick he knew well, she thinks. And then she has an idea. She takes the lizard potion from Cedric's magic bag and spills it on herself.

"Sofia's a lizard!" James shouts.
In a flash, Cedric cries, "Lizardo chango!"
And – Poof!
– Sofia is back, unharmed.

"You saved Sofia's life!" King Roland cries. "That was magnificent. Thank you!"

"I saved her life?" Cedric asks, blushing as his audience claps.

"You did that on purpose," Cedric whispers to Sofia. Sofia smiles. "It's the one trick I knew you could do no matter how nervous you were."

Cedric's next trick is the invisibility potion! "It's a trick I've been planning for many, many years," he says, raising his wand.

But then he sees Sofia's smiling face. He lowers
his arm...and pours the potion on Clover instead!
Everyone, including King Magnus, is impressed.
"Cedric is a great sorcerer!" he declares.

Back in Cedric's workshop, Sofia gives her friend a gold star. "It was fun being your apprentice," she says. "Good night, Mr. Cedric."

Cedric watches her leave and then turns to Wormwood. "Oh, Wormy," he says. "We can always take over the kingdom tomorrow."